Vampires Don't Wear Polka Dots

by Debbie Dadey and Marcia Jones

illustrated by John Steven Gurney

A
LITTLE APPLE
PAPERBACK

SCHOLASTIC INC.

New York   Toronto   London   Auckland   Sydney

*To Steve and Eric for your support,
and to children everywhere for your
inspiration.*

M.T.J. and D.D.

ISBN 0-590-43411-X

36 35 34 33 32 31 30 29 28 27 26 25   8 9/9 0 1 2/0

Printed in the U.S.A.   40

First Scholastic printing, October 1990

1

A New Teacher

"Poor Mrs. Deedee," said Melody. "I feel sorry for her." A couple of other girls in the third-grade classroom at Bailey Elementary School agreed.

"She got what she deserved." Eddie, the class bully, was a tall kid with curly red hair.

Melody turned to Eddie. "You shouldn't have been so mean to her. If you had been nicer she wouldn't have gone crazy!"

"It's not my fault," Eddie said. "Nobody else was very nice to her either."

It was true. There was not an innocent person in the whole class. Every student there had talked out loud or thrown paper wads or done something to drive their teacher crazy. Mrs. Deedee had not actually gone nuts, but she had quit her job after she found her top desk drawer full of shaving cream.

She had been looking for a pencil when she stuck her hands in the mint-scented shaving cream. "I can't stand it anymore!" Mrs. Deedee screamed. She held her hands up like a surgeon and looked around the room. A wild look came into her eyes.

"I don't know who did this, but I want

you to know that you will pay for it. Someday, you'll get yours! Somebody, somewhere, will make you pay!" She laughed a cackling kind of laugh and left the room.

No one in the third grade had seen Mrs. Deedee since, but it was rumored that she had moved to a small town in the farthest corner of Alaska.

Today, the third grade of Bailey Elementary was getting their new teacher. No one had seen her yet and everyone was worried.

"What if we get a male wrestler?" Melody twisted one of her jet black pigtails. "My cousin's teacher moved away, and they got this male wrestler for their new teacher."

"Oh, be serious, Melody," Howie laughed and wrinkled his freckle-covered nose. "Wrestlers don't become teachers!"

"I *am* serious. He weighed at least 300 pounds and had muscles the size of watermelons. He threatened to stuff anybody who misbehaved inside their pencil boxes."

"Did he ever do it?" Howie asked.

"No. He never had to. Nobody ever misbehaved," Melody answered. Everybody agreed that having a male wrestler for a teacher would be a lot worse than having Mrs. Deedee.

A short girl named Liza spoke up. "Maybe we'll get Miss Viola Swamp." Everybody laughed. Viola Swamp was a character in a book they had read.

Liza turned bright red. "Well, we might get her for a teacher and then you'd all be sorry!" That silenced everyone. Viola Swamp was the strictest, meanest teacher in the whole world. If they got somebody like her, they would all be doomed.

"Don't worry," Eddie bragged. "I can

take care of any teacher — even a male wrestler!"

Footsteps from out in the hall made everybody scramble for their seats. An uneasy quiet settled over the class as the footsteps stopped in front of the third-grade room. A couple of students took deep breaths as the doorknob slowly turned.

2

Mrs. Jeepers

Their principal, Mr. Davis, walked into the classroom with a beautiful lady. "Good morning, students," the principal said. Mr. Davis looked something like an egg with two legs. He wore dark-rimmed glasses and was completely bald. "I would like to introduce you to your new teacher, Mrs. Jeepers."

Mrs. Jeepers smiled at the class and said in a strange accent, "It is very nice to meet you, boys and girls. I am sure we are going to have a good year together."

Some of the girls in the back of the room giggled at her accent and Mr. Davis looked at them sternly. "I am sure that no one in the class will give you trouble, Mrs. Jeepers. If they do, I want you to let me know."

"Thank you, Mr. Davis. I am sure we will be fine." Mrs. Jeepers smiled an odd little half smile.

The door closed with a loud click as Mr. Davis left. All twenty-two children looked at Mrs. Jeepers. She was kind of short and her long red hair was pulled back with a purple barrette. She wore a starched white blouse with a high collar. At the collar was a green brooch the size of a chicken egg. It seemed to glow whenever she moved. Her skirt was black and hung to the tops of her black, laced, pointy-toed boots.

While the class stared at her, Mrs. Jeepers looked around the room. A couple of kids were chewing gum and almost everybody slouched in their chairs. A fat boy picked his nose and a girl in the back combed her long blonde hair. Loose papers and books were scattered all over the floor.

Mrs. Jeepers cleared her throat and spoke. "I am glad to be your teacher and I think we should start off by laying the groundwork. There are some rules I expect you to follow."

A few kids in the class groaned.

"Do not worry. They are not difficult rules. They are probably ones that you have already been following. We will start with the most important ones." With that, Mrs. Jeepers proceeded to write three rules on the board.

1. Act nicely to teachers and fellow students.
2. Talk at appropriate times.
3. Walk.

Eddie waved his hand in the air. "What if we don't follow those rules? What'll happen then?"

Mrs. Jeepers smiled and flashed her

green eyes. "I hope you never have to find out."

With the rules out of the way, Mrs. Jeepers started classwork. Everybody remembered Mr. Davis' warning for a little while and the morning went smoothly. Mrs. Jeepers seemed to be a pretty fun teacher. During social studies she even told the class about her home country.

Mrs. Jeepers started speaking very softly. "I come from the country of Romania." She picked up a globe and spun it to show where Romania was located.

"Jeepers doesn't sound like a Romanian name to me," Eddie said.

Mrs. Jeepers flashed her eyes in his direction. "My real name is too difficult to pronounce. I changed it when I came to America."

All the students leaned forward to hear her better. Even Eddie, who always tried to act as if he weren't paying attention, leaned on his elbows and listened.

"Romania is a small country bordered by Russia and the Black Sea. I grew up on my family's estate at the foot of the Transylvanian Alps. It was a wonderful life until . . ."

"Until what?" Liza blurted.

Mrs. Jeepers flashed her green eyes. "Until my family was forced to leave."

"Why did you have to leave?" Melody asked.

Mrs. Jeepers gently touched her brooch. "Oh, that is not important now," she said with a little half smile. Then she dismissed the class for recess.

3

The Haunted House

A group of third-graders met under the giant oak tree on the playground. The tree's branches were like a tent above them. A breeze whispered through the golden leaves.

"I think she's strange," Melody said. "Have you noticed her odd little smile?"

"I think she smiles because she's nice. And her accent is really neat!" Liza said.

"I think her accent is freaky. And what about that Romanian story?" Howie asked.

Carey nodded her head. "Why do you think her family had to leave? Do you think they're criminals?"

Melody's eyes got big. "Maybe they're jewel thieves. That's probaby where she got that huge brooch she wears. Have you noticed how she keeps rubbing it?"

Eddie reached over and pulled Melody's ponytail. "Yeah, she could even be a murderer," he snickered. "I bet she murdered all the kids in her last class!"

Howie gave Eddie a push. "Be serious! We need to decide how we're going to treat Mrs. Jeepers!"

Eddie rolled his eyes. "I think you guys need to get serious. Mrs. Jeepers is just an ordinary teacher with a strange-sounding voice. As a matter-of-fact, I think she's an old-fashioned softie!"

"What do you mean?" Melody asked. "What makes you think she's a softie?"

Eddie leaned against the rough trunk of the giant oak and looked each one of his friends in the eyes. "Didn't you notice that she never once raised her voice today? And what about those sissy rules on the board. No mean teacher would think about using rules like that. She

14

didn't mention one thing about pushing, hitting, or spitting. Any teacher who knows what she's doing would have really laid down the law. But all she did was smile that silly grin!"

"So, what are you getting at?" Melody asked.

"It's simple," Eddie said. "We can get rid of this one like we got rid of Mrs. Deedee."

His friends looked at Eddie. Slowly, Howie started to shake his head. "I don't know, Eddie. This time you may be wrong. Mrs. Jeepers might surprise us!"

Later, on their way home, Eddie, Melody, and some of the other third-graders were walking down Delaware Boulevard.

"Yuck, somebody is moving into the Clancy estate. You couldn't get me to move in there for a million bucks!" Melody shuddered.

"It sure is creepy looking. I bet it's haunted with ghosts and vampires." Eddie pretended to bite a couple of the kids on the neck.

Melody shook her head. "I can't believe anybody would want to live there. They would have to be crazy."

The whole group jumped when a voice came from behind them. "Good afternoon, children. I see you have noticed my new home."

They all turned to see Mrs. Jeepers smiling at them.

"You mean you're going to live here?" Howie asked.

"Yes, is it not lovely? Would you like to come in and see it?" asked Mrs. Jeepers.

"Nooooo, thank you," Melody said quickly. "I mean, I have to get home to do my homework."

"Do not be silly. I did not give you any

homework today." With that, she took Eddie and Melody by their arms and gently pulled them toward the heavy wooden front door. The other kids suddenly heard their mothers calling them and ran home as fast as they could.

"It is so nice to have company. I do get lonely sometimes," Mrs. Jeepers said as she stepped out of the way of two moving men.

"Do you live by yourself, Mrs. Jeepers?" Melody asked.

Mrs. Jeepers smiled and looked at the long wooden box the men were carrying through the basement door. "Well, not exactly alone. But it is quiet most of the time."

Mrs. Jeepers pulled the reluctant pair into the front hall of the big house. A huge cobwebbed-covered chandelier hung from the high ceiling. A massive wooden staircase curved down to meet the dusty

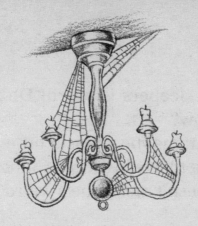

blood-red carpet. Cobwebs clung to the walls and a dusty mist filled the air.

"Is it not lovely?" Mrs. Jeepers asked. "I know it needs some work, but it really has a lot of potential."

"Er, yes, it's real nice," Melody lied.

"Would you like to see the rest of the house?" Mrs. Jeepers asked.

"We'd really like to. Maybe some other time," Eddie said quickly. "You might want to clean up or something. We'll see you tomorrow, Mrs. Jeepers." Eddie grabbed Melody's arm and pulled her out the door.

When they were safe on the other side of the street, Melody glared at Eddie.

"See! Mrs. Jeepers *is* weird! Do you believe us now?"

"All right, maybe she is a little strange for wanting to live in the old Clancy place, but that doesn't mean she's weird," Eddie said.

"I don't know, Eddie," Melody warned. "I think we'd all better watch out for Mrs. Jeepers."

4

Suspicions

Mrs. Jeepers was late for class the next morning. The students sat in their seats and anxiously listened for her footsteps.

"Maybe she quit," Liza suggested.

"Why would she quit?" Eddie asked. "She's only been here one day. She hasn't gotten the full treatment yet!"

"I don't think she quit, either," Howie whispered. "We saw her moving into the Clancy house yesterday!"

"THE CLANCY HOUSE!" several students gasped.

"That place has been empty ever since I can remember," Carey said. "I heard it was haunted!"

"Maybe a ghost ate her," Liza said. "Or maybe she was bitten by a vampire!"

"That's right!" snapped Melody. "I remember seeing the moving men carry a box into the basement yesterday."

"So?" several children chimed.

"So . . . the box was shaped long and thin — like a coffin!"

"She did say she was from Transylvania," Howie said. "And isn't that where Count Dracula lives?"

A ghostly silence filled the room as the doorknob slowly turned. Everyone snapped to attention as Mrs. Jeepers came into the room.

"Good morning, class," Mrs. Jeepers said in her strange accent. "I am sorry to be late. But I did not get much sleep last night."

Melody's eyes grew wide and Howie's mouth dropped open.

"Vampires don't sleep at night," Melody whispered to Liza.

Liza leaned over and said, "Yeah, but vampires don't wear polka dots."

Everyone looked at Mrs. Jeepers. It was true. She didn't look like a vampire today. She had on a bright pink-and-green polka-dotted dress with a bright green ribbon tied in her red hair. Her fingernails were even painted bright green. And at her neck was the green brooch.

"Perhaps we had better start with our lesson," Mrs. Jeepers suggested. "We will begin with arithmetic."

The class opened their books. Not a sound could be heard as she explained the problems and did examples on the board. Eddie looked at his friends. They were being too quiet.

Eddie wadded his math paper. The crinkling of the paper broke the silence. Several of his friends gasped as they turned to Eddie. Mrs. Jeepers didn't even flinch.

Tap-tap-tap. Eddie drummed his pencil on his desk. He glanced at his friends and noticed that some of them were moving their lips as though they were praying. Mrs. Jeepers just wrote another problem on the board.

Eddie started making goldfish noises with his mouth. The students sitting near

him sunk low in their seats, but Mrs. Jeepers didn't notice. He watched the minute hand of the clock go around three times. Still, Mrs. Jeepers ignored him. His mouth began to get dry and his jaws felt as if he had been chewing a super-big wad of bubble gum for hours. This was too much. Eddie wasn't used to being ignored, especially by a teacher.

Eddie stopped making goldfish noises and watched as Mrs. Jeepers showed the class how to work the problems for their assignment. He watched as she neatly wrote one number after another. Suddenly, an idea came to him. He held his math book high in the air. Then he let it go.

KA-BLAM! Everyone in the class jumped as the book fell to the floor with a thud. Everyone except Mrs. Jeepers.

Oh so slowly, Mrs. Jeepers ran her

fingernails down the blackboard. Cold chills escaped down Eddie's neck and back. The screeching of her fingernails on the blackboard made everyone forget about Eddie's book falling to the floor.

Turning, Mrs. Jeepers peered straight at Eddie. Calmly, and almost in a whisper, she spoke in her strange accent, "That is quite enough."

5

Hip Wiggles

Eddie couldn't believe how well the class was behaving. It really bothered him. Nobody had thrown a paper wad or spitball for days. It was as if Mrs. Jeepers had turned everyone into a goody-goody. Everyone but Eddie. Eddie hated being good. It made him sick. He was just itching to cause some trouble.

He leaned over and poked Howie in the ribs. "How about switching everybody's pencils when they're not looking?"

"Shhh! Mrs. Jeepers might hear," Howie warned.

"Well, how about . . ." Eddie started.

"Shhh!" Howie shook his head no.

Eddie turned away in disgust. Howie used to be so much fun. Now he was just another student under Mrs. Jeepers' goodness spell.

Eddie reached in front of him and pulled one of Melody's pigtails.

"Ow! Quit that," Melody whispered.

"Bet you can't make me," Eddie dared as he pulled the other pigtail.

"If you don't quit, I'll tell Mrs. Jeepers," Melody warned.

"So, see if I care," Eddie sneered, but he stopped pulling her pigtails. He tried to work on his science assignment but his heart wasn't in it.

Eddie walked up to the front of the room and wiggled his hips, making a couple of girls giggle. He stuck his already sharp pencil in the pencil sharpener. He turned the sharpener quickly and kept time by wiggling his hips. A few more people giggled, but not enough to make Eddie happy.

Eddie dropped his pencil and crawled all over the front of the classroom looking for it. He started bumping into chairs and feeling things as if he were blind. People were really watching now and some were laughing. Eddie was having a great time until he felt a hand on his shoulder.

The hand had bright green fingernails and it squeezed his shoulder, lifting him off the floor. All of a sudden, Eddie found himself looking into Mrs. Jeepers' eyes. Her green eyes flashed and then she said softly, "That is quite enough."

6

A Dare

Eddie stayed quiet for the rest of the day, and he kept an eye on Mrs. Jeepers. The rest of the class watched her, too. Something was suspicious about their new teacher, no doubt about it. Nobody could forget the way her eyes had flashed at Eddie.

At last the bell rang and Mrs. Jeepers smiled her odd little half smile. "Class is dismissed for today," she said.

Liza waved her hand in the air. "What about homework, Mrs. Jeepers? Don't you want to assign anything?"

Nobody groaned or said a word. Mrs. Jeepers looked at her class. They were sitting up straight, waiting for her reply.

"I believe we have worked enough for today. I do not think a homework assignment will be necessary. You are dismissed."

Several students sighed with relief, but nobody said a word until they had left the building.

Once outside, they gathered around the old oak tree. A few leaves drifted to the ground and crunched under the children's feet.

"That lady is definitely weird," Melody said. "I don't like the way her eyes flashed at Eddie. I think she's trouble."

Howie nodded. "I think we've definitely met our match."

"Aw, what are you guys talking about?" Eddie said. "You're acting like a bunch of sissies!"

"Then how come you acted so scared of her today?" Howie asked.

"I wasn't scared. No teacher can scare me!" Eddie shouted.

"If you weren't scared, then why did

you give up?" Melody asked.

"Yeah, and why did your face turn as white as cotton when she touched your shoulder at the pencil sharpener? How do you explain that?" Howie asked.

"I wasn't scared," Eddie sniffed. "I just didn't feel good, that's all. I think I'm probably coming down with the flu."

Melody sat down on the grass in a fit of giggles. "Eddie, you were scared, plain and simple."

Eddie's face wasn't white, now. It turned as red as an apple. "I am *not* scared of Mrs. Jeepers," he said. "And I'll be glad to prove it to you!"

His friends stopped laughing and looked long and hard at Eddie.

"Are you sure you know what you're saying, Eddie?" Liza asked softly. "We'd all understand if you want to change your mind."

"I am not a sissy like you guys and I'll

prove it. You just tell me how!"

Howie was the first one to speak. He talked slowly, choosing his words with care. "I'll tell you what, Eddie. If you find out what's in that big box in her basement, then we'll know you're not bluffing."

Everybody looked at Howie.

"Are you crazy, Howie?" Liza asked. "He'd have to sneak into her basement to find out what's in that box!"

"Exactly," Howie said. "But I think Eddie's too chicken to do it."

"Am not," Eddie snapped. "I'll find out what's in that box."

Melody looked thoughtfully at Eddie. "How will we know that Eddie really does it?"

"What's the matter, don't you trust me?" Eddie sneered.

"Of course not," Melody said. "Nobody does!"

"Well, if that's how you feel, you can come with me. Then you'll know I'm not lying! Or are you a scaredy-cat?"

Melody glared at Eddie. "I can do anything you can. We'll go tonight," she said. Then she turned and walked away.

7

The Basement

That night Eddie sneaked out of his house and met Melody in front of the Clancy place.

"Where have you been?" Melody hissed. "I've been waiting for ten minutes!"

"Well, I had to wait for my dad to sack out. Did you bring your flashlight?"

Melody patted a big bulge in her coat pocket. "It's right here. Let's go."

Eddie paused for a minute to pull his turtleneck high up on his neck. He looked at the old house. Most of the shutters were missing and every window was dark. A streetlight cast shadows on the house. Eddie was sure he saw bats circling around the light. He took a deep breath and said, "Ready when you are!"

Together, they sneaked up to the basement door. One of the glass panes in the door was cracked and another was completely broken. Eddie reached through the broken window and unlocked the door. The children froze as the door squeaked open, but the rest of the house remained deathly still.

Melody's hand trembled as she pulled out her flashlight. "Let's get this over with," she whispered. "This place gives me the creeps."

"OK," Eddie said. "You go first, you've got the flashlight."

"Here, you can have it." Melody shoved the flashlight into Eddie's chest.

Thanks a lot," Eddie said. "You're a true friend." Eddie shone the light into the dark hole leading to the basement. Cobwebs brushed their faces as they crept down the steps.

"Yuk! It smells like wet socks in here," Melody complained.

"Maybe it's a dead body," Eddie said.

"Be serious," Melody whispered.

"I am," Eddie said.

Eddie shone the light all around the dusty basement. Broken chairs and cardboard boxes littered the damp floor. The long wooden box rested in the far corner.

"There it is," Eddie whispered.

"Do you really think it's a coffin?" Melody shuddered.

"Maybe. Do you still want to go through with this?"

"Are you chickening out?" Melody asked hopefully.

"Not me! But if you want to I'll understand," Eddie said.

"I'm no chicken, Eddie," Melody said.

"Neither am I!" Eddie picked his way around the junk in the basement to the box. Melody followed silently. They stood, peering down at the box. It *was* long enough for a grown man to lie down inside.

"Do you want to open it or shall I?" Eddie asked.

"We'll do it together," Melody answered.

They placed their hands on the lid and lifted.

"Gee, this thing won't budge," Melody gasped.

"Maybe it's locked." Eddie peered at the lid, looking for a latch. "I don't see a lock."

Melody felt around the edges to see if she could find the latch. "Me neither. You don't suppose it's locked from the inside, do you?"

"Don't be so stupid. How could it be locked from the inside? That wouldn't be any good unless . . ."

"Unless someone was inside to unlock it," Melody finished for him.

Melody looked at Eddie and Eddie looked at Melody. Then they both looked at the box. Neither of them said a word. In the chilling silence they heard a thump.

"What was that?" Melody jumped and grabbed hold of Eddie's arm.

"Shhh! I don't know. But whatever it was, I didn't like it!"

"Where did it come from?" Melody asked.

"I think it came from the box," Eddie gasped.

"Let's get out of here, Eddie. Before we become vampire bait." Melody grabbed Eddie's hand and started pulling him toward the door. They dodged broken furniture, jumped over boxes, and flew up the steps. They didn't bother to close the door as they rushed into the cool night air.

Safely across the street, Melody and Eddie stopped to catch their breaths. "Look!" Eddie pointed toward the Clancy house. A light shone through an upstairs window. They dived behind a bush and watched as a series of lights flickered on. A ghostly looking woman opened the front door and peered in their direction. Was it their imagination — or did they really see something green flashing in the darkness of the night?

8

Chickening Out

"So what was in the box?" Liza asked.

"Was it a body?" Howie wondered.

"Or was it a vampire?" Carey asked.

The small group of students were huddled under the towering oak tree. It was early, at least fifteen minutes before school was to start. A nippy breeze stung their faces and a fine layer of frost covered the ground.

Eddie and Melody looked at each other nervously. They hadn't decided what to tell their friends about the night before.

"Hey, I bet they chickened out," Howie said. "Look at them, they can't say what was in the box."

"I bet they didn't even go last night," Carey said.

"We did so!" snapped Melody. "We both sneaked out of our houses and went to her house and into her basement."

"We aren't chickens!" added Eddie.

"Then what did you find?" demanded Howie.

"Well . . . the basement was really a mess," Eddie began. "It took us a while just to find the box. But when we started to open it, we heard a noise come from inside."

"Inside the box?" Howie exclaimed. "Did you open it?"

"No," Melody admitted. "But we tried. I think it was locked from the inside. And when we heard the noise, we figured we'd better get out of there!"

"That's it! Mrs. Jeepers must be a vampire. I bet that's where she sleeps at night," Carey gasped.

"I'm not so sure about that," Eddie said. "After we left, we hid in a bush. A light came on upstairs. Pretty soon Mrs. Jeepers opened the front door. If she was the vampire, then who turned on the light upstairs?"

"Besides," Howie added, "vampires don't sleep at night."

The children thought hard for a few minutes.

"Her husband must be a vampire and she takes care of him," Liza said. "Maybe he doesn't come out 'til midnight!"

"I bet her husband is Count Dracula, and he has her under his spell." Melody was so excited she was almost yelling.

"Good morning, children. What is all the excitement about?" Mrs. Jeepers had come up behind them without their even knowing it. She had on a black dress with a high collar, and a bat bracelet. And she still wore the strange green brooch.

Melody turned bright red. "Oh, nothing, Mrs. Jeepers. We were just talking about a television show we watched last night."

"Oh, I never watch television. I always have too much to do," Mrs. Jeepers said. "It is time for school to begin. We had better go inside." She started walking toward the school with Liza beside her.

"I've never seen a bat bracelet before," Liza told her. "Where'd you get it?"

"My husband gave it to me."

"Where is he?" Liza asked.

"Well, I am not exactly married anymore."

"How come?" Howie asked. "Are you divorced? My parents are divorced."

"Not exactly. My husband died," Mrs. Jeepers said.

"Oh, I'm sorry," Liza said sadly.

"It is quite all right. Sometimes I feel as if he is still with me," Mrs. Jeepers said cheerfully.

Everybody stared at Mrs. Jeepers. It seemed as if their suspicions were turning out to be true!

9

The Boss

The students filed into the room and silently took their seats. Sitting up straight, they waited for Mrs. Jeepers to begin class. She stood stiffly and looked at every student in the room.

"When I was a child in Romania, we were taught to be respectful of all others," she began. "It was a reward in itself when we pleased our elders. We only needed to be told once to keep the floors free from litter, or to keep our appearance neat."

Mrs. Jeepers paused to glance at the floor. Papers were scattered around nearly every desk. She cleared her throat once and then waited.

Some students looked uncomfortably at each other while a few others tucked in their shirts and swallowed wads of chewing gum. Then very slowly, they leaned down and scooped up trash, pencils, and erasers so that the floor was clean. Without waiting to be asked, Howie walked to the front of the room and picked up the trash can. He kept his eyes glued to the floor as he walked up and down the aisles collecting trash.

"Thank you, class, particularly Howie. I am sure I will not need to remind you again about the appearance of the room or of yourselves." Mrs. Jeepers' green eyes flashed and her brooch seemed to glow dully.

"Forgive me if I seem to be grouchy today," Mrs. Jeepers continued. "I had the unfortunate experience of having prowlers enter my home last night. They disturbed my sleep." She peered around the room, letting her green eyes rest on

Melody and Eddie for a split second. Then she blinked and smiled. "However, no harm was done and I am willing to forget the experience. I feel sure that it will never happen again! Now, please open your English books and we will begin our lesson."

Melody's hands trembled and she peeked at Eddie. He had his attention glued to his book. No one made a sound as Mrs. Jeepers began teaching the class about nouns and verbs.

The rest of the morning passed quickly. By lunchtime the third-graders had finished all their assignments and were ready for a break. In the cafeteria they quietly began to eat their lunches.

"What's wrong with you guys?" Ben asked from the next table. Ben was a fourth-grader in Mr. Powers' room. He was known for his loud voice and for the dumb jokes he told. "You're all so quiet today."

"Shhh! Mrs. Jeepers might hear you," Howie whispered.

"So what? Talking is allowed in the cafeteria. Don't tell me you're actually scared of a teacher!" Ben laughed and poked Eddie in the ribs.

Eddie washed down the rest of his peanut-butter-and-jelly sandwich with a swig of milk. "Cut it out, Ben."

"What's the matter?" Ben started to laugh. "Don't tell me you're turning into a teacher's pet!"

"No way!" Eddie hissed.

"Whatever you say, sissy," Ben teased, as both the classes stood up to empty their lunch trays.

Eddie stuck out his foot to trip Ben. He smiled when Ben's tray went crashing to the floor. "That'll teach you to call me a

sissy," Eddie snapped. He hurried to line up with the rest of his class before Ben could say anything else.

Once the third grade was back in their room, Eddie started thinking. Things had definitely gotten out of hand. He wasn't used to a teacher making him behave. This had to stop. He was determined to show Mrs. Jeepers who was boss.

10

Freeze

Eddie went into action. He knocked something off every desk he walked by, scattering papers everywhere. He stuffed a wad of bubble gum in his mouth and started popping bubbles loudly. Melody looked at him in disbelief.

"Are you crazy?" she whispered.

"I know exactly what I'm doing," Eddie said as he blew another big bubble.

Melody shrugged. "It's your funeral."

Mrs. Jeepers paid no attention to Eddie. She was too busy grading papers.

Eddie decided to give her something to notice. He slouched down in his chair and kicked his shoes off. Then he propped his feet up on the seat in front of him. Once he was comfortable, he started stretching his gum to see how long he could make it. When it finally broke, he twirled the slimy strand around his finger. Mrs. Jeepers still did not look up.

This was getting ridiculous. Then he had an inspiration. He took three giant gulps of air, put his head down, and let out a deep burp.

Howie laughed out loud but stopped when Mrs. Jeepers cleared her throat. Eddie stuffed the gum back into his mouth and with precise timing, managed to pop a bubble and burp at the same time.

A few kids around him snickered. Eddie was feeling good now. He was ready for his grand finale. He looked around to make sure everyone was watching. Then he blew the biggest bubble he'd ever blown. Just as he was ready to suck it back into his mouth, he saw Mrs. Jeepers through the filmy pink bubble.

Her eyes flashed and she gently rubbed her brooch. She held up her hand and flicked her finger in Eddie's direction. Instantly the bubble popped. Gobs of

pink, sticky gum covered Eddie's face and hair.

Mrs. Jeepers smiled her odd little half smile and then went back to grading papers. A few kids stared with their mouths hanging open. Mrs. Jeepers hadn't even moved from her desk but she had made Eddie's bubble pop!

As Eddie started pulling stringy globs from his eyebrows, he heard Howie and Melody giggling.

"What's so funny," he said, pulling gum from the tip of his ear.

Howie turned back to his work but Melody couldn't stop laughing.

"She really got you that time," Melody whispered between giggles.

"What are you talking about? It was just a coincidence!" Eddie snapped.

Melody shook her head as though she didn't believe him, then turned back to her work. Eddie finished scraping gum from his nose and chin. He decided to cut the rest of the gum from his hair when he got home. He drummed his fingers on his desk while he thought about what had happened. Things certainly had not gone the way he planned. Instead of getting Mrs. Jeepers upset, he had ended up being embarrassed in front of all his friends. This called for drastic measures.

Eddie was still trying to think of something to do when Mrs. Jeepers cleared her throat. "You have been working very nicely this afternoon. I have decided that we might play math relays for the rest of the day."

Everybody clapped their hands. Math relays were a great way to practice their multiplication tables. Two teams quickly lined up. Mrs. Jeepers stood at the front of each line and held up a flash card. Several kids were hopping up and down as they tried to think of answers while others were trying to count on their fingers.

They had gone two rounds before Eddie came up with a brainstorm. This was the perfect time to cause trouble. Even though it wasn't his turn, he yelled out the wrong answer on purpose. Mrs. Jeepers flashed her eyes at him, but continued holding up the card. The next time she showed a card, Eddie burped. His teammates stopped long enough to glare at him.

It was Carey's and Liza's turn. Carey held both her hands in front of her as if she were praying. Liza was so excited she hopped on one foot and shook her arms as if they were wet. Eddie jabbed Howie and pointed at Liza.

"Look at her," he laughed. "She looks like she's trying to fly. Watch!" Eddie started jumping and flapping his arms in the air. He bumped into several students and knocked down a chair. He didn't even notice Mrs. Jeepers.

Mrs. Jeepers rubbed her brooch until it shone bright green. "That is quite enough," she said rather sternly.

Eddie acted as though he hadn't heard a thing, but there was something about her brooch that caught his eye. He stopped jumping just to watch it. The more Mrs. Jeepers rubbed it, the more it seemed to glow. He couldn't take his eyes off it.

"We may continue our game now," Mrs. Jeepers informed the class. "We will no longer be rudely interrupted."

With serious expressions, the students turned back to Mrs. Jeepers. They no longer were excited about the game. As a matter-of-fact, it was sort of creepy because they kept having to step around Eddie. He stayed rooted in the same spot, staring at Mrs. Jeepers' green brooch for the rest of the game.

Finally, the bell rang. As the class lined up, Mrs. Jeepers walked over to Eddie. She placed her left hand on her brooch, then snapped her fingers in front of his face.

"Hey," he said loudly. "Aren't we going to play anymore?"

11

No Ordinary Teacher

The third-grade class gathered outside in their usual place — under the big oak tree.

"Did you see what Mrs. Jeepers did to Eddie?" Melody squealed.

"I couldn't believe it," Liza said. "Are you OK, Eddie?"

"What are you guys talking about? She didn't do a thing to me all day. She let me get away with murder!"

"Eddie, she hypnotized you into a frozen Popsicle and you didn't even know it!" Howie shouted.

"You guys are crazier than you look. Mrs. Jeepers is a wimp and I can prove it. Tomorrow I'll give her a day she'll never forget."

"Eddie, are you crazy?" Howie asked.

"Mrs. Jeepers is a witch or a vampire or something. There's no telling what she'll do to you if she really gets mad."

"Mad, smad. Just wait until tomorrow. Mrs. Jeepers will run out of that room faster than you can say Transylvania." Eddie turned and stomped off.

Melody looked at Howie. "You know, maybe we should do something about Mrs. Jeepers. I mean, it is definitely not normal to hypnotize a student during math class."

"I know," agreed Howie. "But who could we tell? Mr. Davis would probably laugh us right out of his office."

Melody nodded her head. "Either that or put us in a nuthouse."

"What about your parents? Would they believe you?" Howie asked.

"No, my mom would just tell me to stop exaggerating, and I'd probably get in trouble for telling lies about my teacher."

"Yeah, me too," Howie sighed. "It's crazy. Here we are trying to save our class from total destruction by a mad woman and nobody will believe us!"

"I guess we're just gonna have to depend on ourselves," Melody said.

"I just hope we'll be a match for Mrs. Jeepers," said Howie.

"Me, too," Melody said softly.

The next morning Howie and Melody were the first to meet under the big oak tree. Howie pulled out a large book from his bookbag.

"Look what I got from the public library last night." Howie held up a book called *Vampires and Witches: The True Story*.

"Did you find out anything?" Melody asked.

"I stayed up late and read the whole section on vampires. I found out what we need to do to protect ourselves if Mrs. Jeepers really is some kind of vampire," Howie said.

"What do we need to do?" Melody took the book and started flipping through it.

Howie spoke with authority. "There are a couple of things vampires can't stand. One is a cross." Howie pulled open his jacket to reveal a huge gold cross necklace that hung around his neck. "Another thing they don't like is garlic," he continued.

Melody's eyes grew wide. "Did you bring some garlic, too?"

"We didn't have any real garlic at home so I brought this." Howie held up a small plastic bottle labeled garlic salt.

"Do you think that'll work?" Melody asked.

"Well, it's worth a try. Will you go with me to sprinkle it around the classroom?" Howie asked as he gathered up his stuff.

"Me?" Melody squeaked. "Why don't we wait for somebody else to come and help?"

"Because if we wait too long, Mrs. Jeepers will be there," Howie said impatiently. "And if we don't do it today, she might turn Eddie into a frog — or hypnotize him forever!"

"I guess you're right," Melody agreed reluctantly. Eddie wasn't exactly her favorite person, but she still didn't want anything bad to happen to him.

They tiptoed into the school and held their breath as they opened the classroom door.

"Good, she's not here yet," Howie whispered. Without another word he started sprinkling the garlic salt all around the room, especially around Eddie's desk. He had used every last drop when the door to the classroom opened suddenly. In walked Mrs. Jeepers.

"Good morning, children," Mrs. Jeepers smiled. "This is quite a surprise. What are you two doing here so early?"

Howie quickly slipped the empty bottle of garlic salt into his pocket and answered. "We thought we might be able to help you with something."

Melody quickly added, "Yeah, we wanted to help you pick up paper and straighten books and stuff."

Mrs. Jeepers rubbed her brooch softly. "Why, how very thoughtful of you. You can get started right away."

Melody and Howie exchanged a look of relief and started cleaning the room.

12

Ker-choo

As soon as Eddie arrived, trouble began. "Phew, somebody stinks!" he yelled. "Who had spaghetti for breakfast?"

Howie and Melody gestured to Eddie to be quiet, but he ignored them. Instead, he skipped to the back of the room and dumped the contents of his bookbag. At least twenty paper airplanes floated to the floor. As the rest of the kids entered, Eddie took aim. Paper planes soared diz-

zily around the room and then drifted to the floor.

Mrs. Jeepers was too busy blowing her nose to notice Eddie's planes. But as soon as the class figured out what Eddie was doing, they wadded up his planes into tight balls and tossed them in the garbage.

"Hey! What are you guys doing?" Eddie complained.

Several children glared at Eddie and hissed, "Shhhh!"

They all went to their seats, sat up straight, and gave Mrs. Jeepers their full attention. But not Eddie. He took all the books off the shelves and scattered them on the floor. He didn't notice that Mrs. Jeepers had gone into a sneezing fit.

"Ker-choo, ker-choo, KER-CHOO," she wheezed. "Excuse me, class. Something seems to be making me sneeze . . . ker-choo!" Mrs. Jeepers pulled a tissue from the box on her desk and blew her nose.

Her eyes were red and tears crept from their corners.

Liza waved her hand in the air. "When I have an allergy attack my mother does major house cleaning. She says it's the dust and cat hair that makes me sneeze. Maybe I should go get the custodian."

Melody leaned over and pinched Liza. But she sat back up when she noticed Mrs. Jeepers looking her way.

"Ker-choo," Mrs. Jeepers said. Then she shook her head. "That won't be necessary, Liza. I believe I know what is making me sneeze. There's only one thing it could be. I just cannot imagine how garlic has gotten into this room."

Howie sucked in his breath real fast, while Melody started digging through the books in her desk. Neither one noticed how Mrs. Jeepers' teary eyes were glowing green.

Meanwhile, Eddie had stopped taking

the books off the shelves. He glanced at Mrs. Jeepers and watched while she blew her nose again. Her allergy was interfering with all his pranks. As far as he could tell, Mrs. Jeepers wasn't even able to see him through her tissues.

Eddie stepped over the books on the floor and headed for his desk. He pulled a few pigtails and pinched a few ears on his way. He stretched and pretended to yawn before slumping to his desk. "So are you sick or something?" he hollered. "Sick people shouldn't come to school. You're exposing us to all your cootie germs!"

Howie covered his eyes and Liza gasped. But Mrs. Jeepers acted as if she hadn't heard a thing. She turned and began to write the morning assignments on the board. She had to stop every so often to sneeze, but soon the board was full and the class got busy.

Eddie looked around him with disgust. The room was so quiet that he could hear pencils scratching on paper. The only other sound was Mrs. Jeepers' sniffles.

By lunchtime, Eddie had already sharpened all of his pencils and a few of his crayons until they were nubs. He had dumped the entire contents of his desk on the floor and kicked them halfway across the room. He had hummed, whistled, and burped until his mouth hurt. But Mrs. Jeepers had been too busy blowing her nose to pay any attention to him. As he followed the rest of the class to the cafeteria, he made his brain work double time trying to think of ways to make her notice him.

Eddie got his lunch tray and sat next to Howie and Melody. "What's wrong with everybody? Don't tell me you're turning into super-students. I've been trying all day to drive Mrs. Jeepers batty.

You guys haven't helped one bit!"

Melody sadly shook her head. "Eddie, can't you get it through your thick skull? Mrs. Jeepers is not ordinary. She's some kind of vampire or witch. If you're not careful, she just might turn you into a frog."

Eddie giggled hysterically. "You've been watching too much TV! There are no such things as vampires or witches."

"Well, if that's true, then tell me why Mrs. Jeepers can't stand the garlic I sprinkled around the room?" Howie asked. "According to a book I got at the library, vampires are repulsed by garlic!"

"Well, I think garlic is repulsive and I'm not a vampire. So that doesn't prove anything," Eddie snapped. "But I do know that this teacher has got to go. So far she's made us clean up the room, get our work done, and be quiet in class. Before you know it, she'll have us actually learning! We've got to do something about her, and fast. And if you're not going to help, I'll just have to get rid of her myself!" With that, Eddie grabbed his tray and stormed away.

Melody shook her head and pushed her tray away. "All of a sudden I'm not too hungry," she moaned.

"Me neither," agreed Howie. "But I *am* scared!"

13

I Have Had Enough

Eddie rushed into the room, ready to cause more trouble. He bumped into the custodian who was just leaving.

"Thank you for sweeping the room, Mr. Dobson. I am sure I will feel much better now," Mrs. Jeepers said.

Melody and Howie gave each other a worried look and then went to their seats. Howie leaned over to Eddie's chair to whisper, "I've got to tell you something."

"Don't bug me, I'm getting ready to bombard Mrs. Jeepers with spitballs."

"But you can't," Howie hissed. "The garlic's gone. Mrs. Jeepers is already feeling better."

It was true. Mrs. Jeepers was no longer blowing her nose or sneezing. Her nose was still a little red, but her green eyes were back to normal. But Eddie was too bent on causing trouble to notice.

He stuck a wad of paper in his mouth and got it good and soggy. With his tongue he rolled it into a small ball. Then, taking careful aim, he let it fly.

SPLAT! It landed right in the middle of Mrs. Jeepers' desk.

"Bingo!" Eddie grinned.

Mrs. Jeepers slowly plucked the spitball from her papers. Her green eyes flashed

as she calmly stood up from her chair. She started to open her mouth to speak when, SPLAT! Another spitball whizzed by her cheek and landed on the blackboard.

Eddie smiled as though he had just won the World Series. He leaned over to Howie and bragged, "See, she's a wimp. She won't do a thing."

Howie didn't answer. He was too busy staring at Mrs. Jeepers. The class was so quiet that when she started speaking in a low voice, it sounded as if she were booming.

"I have had enough."

Her green eyes flashed and her brooch glowed as she deliberately made her way to Eddie. With a trembling hand she grabbed his arm. "Come with me," Mrs. Jeepers demanded.

Eddie whimpered. "I-I-I'm s-s-sorry, Mrs.

J-J-Jeepers. I'll never do it again."

Mrs. Jeepers pulled Eddie from his desk and said *very* quietly, "I will speak with you in the hall this instant."

Everyone watched as Eddie was led into the hall. The door closed with a thud.

"What do you think she'll do to him?" Melody whispered.

"I don't know," Howie gasped. "But I'm glad it's not me!"

All the kids slowly nodded their heads. One by one the whole class started picking up stuff off the floor. While they were at it, they cleaned the blackboards. Then they sat down at their desks and hurried to finish all their work.

They all looked up when the door creaked open. Mrs. Jeepers was back to normal, but Eddie looked as white as a ghost.

* * *

The students met under the oak tree after school. Melody was the first to speak. "What'd she do to you, Eddie?"

"It must've been awful," Howie exclaimed. "You hardly said a word for the rest of the day."

Eddie shook his head, but he didn't speak.

Liza piped up, "You can tell us. Did she grow fangs and bite you on the neck?"

"Don't be stupid," Howie snapped. "She didn't bite him . . . did she?"

All eyes turned to Eddie. With a shudder, he started to speak hoarsely. "I'll only say this, you guys were right. Mrs. Jeepers is no ordinary teacher."

"Is she a vampire?" Liza asked.

Howie grabbed Eddie's arm. "C'mon, you can level with us."

But Eddie wouldn't tell them what happened. All he said was, "I know one thing. I'll never make her mad again."

For the rest of the year, Eddie kept his promise. As a matter of fact, nobody in the third grade at Bailey Elementary ever dared make Mrs. Jeepers mad. And her green brooch never glowed again, although she wore it every day.

On the last day of school, the kids met under the oak tree.

"I can't believe the year's over," Liza said.

"I can't believe we lived through it," Eddie moaned.

"But, you know," Melody said, "Mrs. Jeepers wasn't so bad."

Howie said, "She's really not *that* weird."

Melody laughed. "I can't believe we ever thought she was a vampire!"

"After all," Liza agreed, "vampires don't wear polka dots!"

¿Cuándo llegará mi cumpleaños?

Alejandra Vallejo-Nágera

ALFAGUARA

© De esta edición:
2002, Santillana USA Publishing Company, Inc.
2105 NW 86th Avenue
Miami, FL 33122
© Del texto: 2000, Alejandra Vallejo-Nágera
© De las ilustraciones: 2000, Andrés Guerrero

• Grupo Santillana de Ediciones, S. A.
Torrelaguna, 60. 28043 Madrid
• Aguilar, Altea, Taurus, Alfaguara, S. A. de Ediciones
Beazley, 3860. 1437 Buenos Aires
• Aguilar, Altea, Taurus, Alfaguara, S. A. de C.V.
Avda. Universidad, 767. Col. Del Valle, México D.F. C.P. 03100
• Distribuidora y Editora Aguilar, Altea, Taurus, Alfaguara, S. A.
Calle 80, nº 10-23. Santafe de Bogotá-Colombia

Alfaguara es un sello editorial del **Grupo Santillana**.
Éstas son sus sedes:
ARGENTINA, BOLIVIA, CHILE, COLOMBIA, COSTA RICA,
ECUADOR, EL SALVADOR, ESPAÑA, ESTADOS UNIDOS,
GUATEMALA, MÉXICO, PANAMÁ, PERÚ, PUERTO RICO,
REPÚBLICA DOMINICANA, URUGUAY Y VENEZUELA.

¿Cuándo llegará mi cumpleaños?
ISBN: 1-58986-548-0

Diseño de la colección:
José Crespo, Rosa Marín, Jesús Sanz

Editora:
Marta Higueras Díez

Printed in Colombia by Panamericana Formas e Impresos S.A.

¿Cuándo llegará mi cumpleaños?

Las aventuras de Ricardete y Lola

Alejandra Vallejo-Nágera
Ilustraciones de ANDRÉS GUERRERO

ALFAGUARA
INFANTIL

A Ricardete le gustan sus fiestas
de cumpleaños más que nada
en el mundo...

...pero ha pasado tanto, tanto
tiempo desde su último cumpleaños,
que ya ni se acuerda de las bromas
que le gastó el payaso.

—¡Todos celebran fiestas de cumpleaños
menos yo! —protesta Ricardete.

—Mamá, ¿cuánto falta para mi
cumpleaños? —pregunta Ricardete.

—No seas impaciente. Todavía faltan
muchos meses —contesta.

Pero Ricardete no sabe cuánto
tiempo son muchos meses.

Así que lo pregunta una vez...
...y otra vez...

—¿Cuándo llegará mi cumpleaños?
¿Cuándo llegará? —pregunta
Ricardete sin parar.

—¡En primavera! —responde papá
llevándose las manos a la cabeza.

—En primavera —explica mamá—,
el campo se llena de flores de muchos
colores, y las cigüeñas anidan en lo alto
de las torres.

—Entonces, ahora no puede ser mi
cumpleaños —le dice Ricardete
enfadado.

—Como es verano y hace
mucho calor —explica papá—,
nos ponemos el bañador
y nos damos un chapuzón.

—Entonces, ahora tampoco es mi
cumpleaños —piensa Ricardete.

Después del verano, viene el otoño.
El parque se llena de hojas amarillas
y Ricardete juega con las ardillas.

—Cuando el otoño termine, ¿será
mi cumpleaños? —se pregunta
Ricardete.

Después del otoño, el invierno llega.
—En invierno nieva y la nariz se te
hiela —explica la abuela—, pero ya
falta poco para la primavera.

—¡Y para mi fiesta! —exclama
Ricardete.

Poco a poco el frío se marcha.
Ricardete mira por la ventana y ve
unos puntitos verdes en las ramas...

...y observa que las cigüeñas hacen
mucho ruido, mientras preparan
sus nidos.

—¡Mi cumpleaños se acerca!

—¡Feliz cumpleaños! —le desean
mamá y papá.

Ricardete mira cómo el bizcocho
de chocolate se hincha, y espera
nervioso a sus amigos y amigas.

25

Por fin llegan los invitados
cargados de regalos.
Ricardete recibe tirones de orejas,
y aplausos cuando apaga las velas.

Luego hace carreras de sacos,
rompe la piñata con un palo...

...y sus amigos se marchan agotados.
Entonces Ricardete pregunta acalorado:

—Mamá, papá, ¿cuánto falta
para que vengan los Reyes Magos?